W9-CDB-712

Retold by Marilyn Hirsh

Illustrated by Devis Grebu

PUFFIN BOOKS

To the past and the future
M.H.

To my two dearest Rosalies
D.G.

The art was prepared on Arches watercolor paper using black ink, watercolor, and colored pencil.

PUFFIN BOOKS
Published by the Penguin Group
Viking Penguin Inc., 40 West 23rd Street, New York, New York 10010, U.S.A.
Penguin Books Ltd, 27 Wrights Lane, London W8 5TZ, England
Penguin Books Australia Ltd, Ringwood, Victoria, Australia
Penguin Books Canada Ltd, 2801 John Street, Markham, Ontario, Canada L3R 1B4
Penguin Books (N.Z.) Ltd, 182–190 Wairau Road, Auckland 10, New Zealand

Penguin Books Ltd, Registered Offices: Harmondsworth, Middlesex, England

First published in the United States of America by Viking Penguin Inc., 1986
Published in Picture Puffins 1988
10 9 8 7 6 5 4 3 2
Text copyright © Marilyn Hirsh, 1986
Illustrations copyright © Devis Grebu, 1986
All rights reserved

Library of Congress Cataloging in Publication Data
Hirsh, Marilyn.
Joseph who loved the Sabbath/retold by Marilyn Hirsh : illustrated by Devis Grebu.
p. cm.—(Picture Puffins)
"The source of 'Joseph who loved the Sabbath,' Yosef mokir Shabbat, is eight lines of Aramaic in the Babylonian Talmud (Tractate Shabbat, 119A) ...Marilyn Hirsh has based this retelling on Emanuel bin Gorion's Mimekor Yisrael : classical Jewish folktales"—Colophon.
Summary: Despite his poverty, Joseph celebrated the seventh day with joy.
ISBN 0-14-050670-5
[1. Sabbath—Folklore. 2. Folklore, Jewish.] I. Grebu, Devis, 1933- ill. II. Title. [PZ8.1.H66Jo 1988] 398.2'36'089924—dc19 88-11705 [E]

Printed in Japan by Dai Nippon Printing Co., Ltd.
Set in Trump

Except in the United States of America, this book is sold subject to the condition that it shall not, by way of trade or otherwise, be lent, re-sold, hired out, or otherwise circulated without the publisher's prior consent in any form of binding or cover other than that in which it is published and without a similar condition including this condition being imposed on the subsequent purchaser.

Long ago, there lived a poor man named Joseph. All week long he worked hard so he could buy only the finest things for the Sabbath, the seventh day of the week. He was called "Joseph Who Loves the Sabbath."

Joseph worked on the farm of a rich and greedy man named Sorab. Season after season Joseph plowed, planted, and harvested Sorab's crops.

"What a hot day!" Sorab said to his servant while he watched Joseph work.

Joseph pressed oil from olives, made wine from grapes, and took Sorab's crops to market. He fed the animals and took care of their young.

Sorab did not pay Joseph much money. Joseph asked for more. "I work hard; it's only fair," he explained.

But Sorab refused. He laughed and said, "I can't afford to pay you more. Besides, you crazy fellow, you will only spend it on the Sabbath."

"What better way to spend it?" Joseph replied. So all week Joseph ate barley bread and onions. All week he wore a torn, ragged robe. And Sorab was known throughout the village as a greedy and selfish man.

Every Friday afternoon, Joseph stopped working. It was time to prepare for the Sabbath, the day of rest. First, he cleaned his little house.

Then he took nearly all the money he had earned that week and rushed to the market. Joseph went from stall to stall.

"I'll have a little of your purest oil and some of the best wine," he told a merchant. "Some flour for the Sabbath bread, too."

He called to a farmer, "That plump chicken looks fit for the Sabbath."

"So it is!" the farmer answered. Joseph spent his last coin on the best that the market had to offer.

"Is that a rich man?" asked a stranger in the marketplace.

"Oh, no," said Deborah the weaver, laughing. "That's Joseph Who Loves the Sabbath. He does this *every* week."

At home Joseph roasted the chicken and baked two loaves of Sabbath bread. He put on his robe and his silk prayer shawl with fringes. He took out his Scroll of the Law.

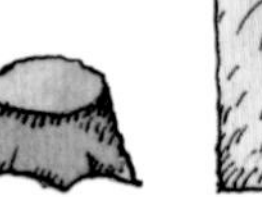

At sundown Joseph lit the oil lamps and said the blessing. He ate the warm bread and the chicken and drank some wine. He stayed up late reading his scroll and singing.

All the next day was the Sabbath, the day of rest, when Joseph did no work. He said prayers, then he shared a meal with some friends and they sang Sabbath songs together. Sometimes he played a game, sometimes he read. Joseph enjoyed the Sabbath.

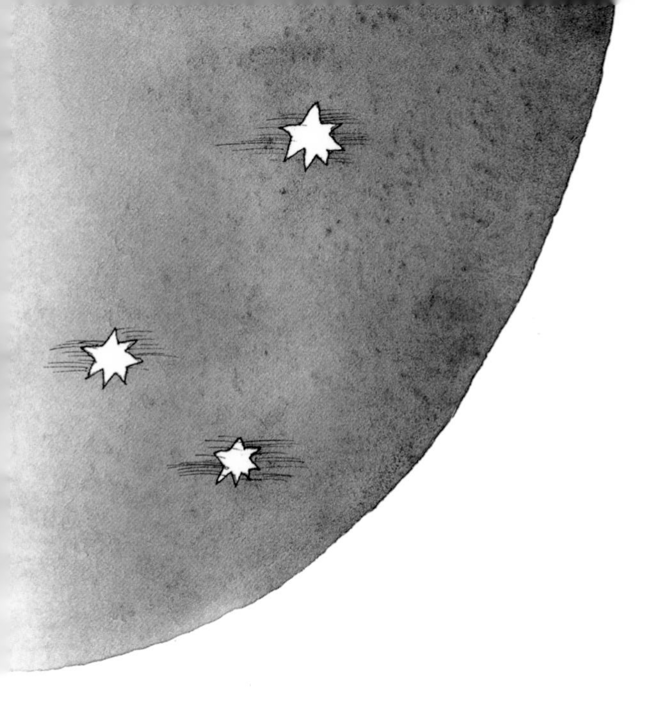

At night, when three stars appeared in the sky, the Sabbath was over. Joseph put away his oil lamps, his silk shawl, and his scroll for another week.

As the days passed, Sorab made Joseph work even harder. No matter how hard Joseph worked, Sorab paid him the same amount of money.

Then, one night, Sorab had a bad dream. A genie appeared to him and said:

All you have, your house and lands
Has been earned by Joseph's hands.
Before this month's full moon grows dim
All you have will go to him.

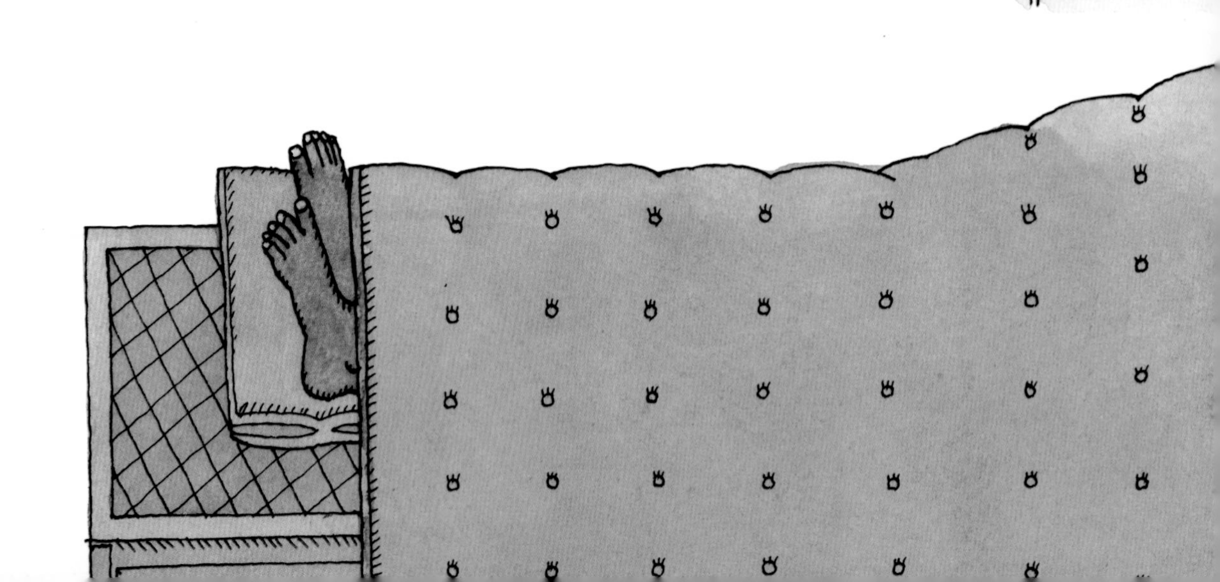

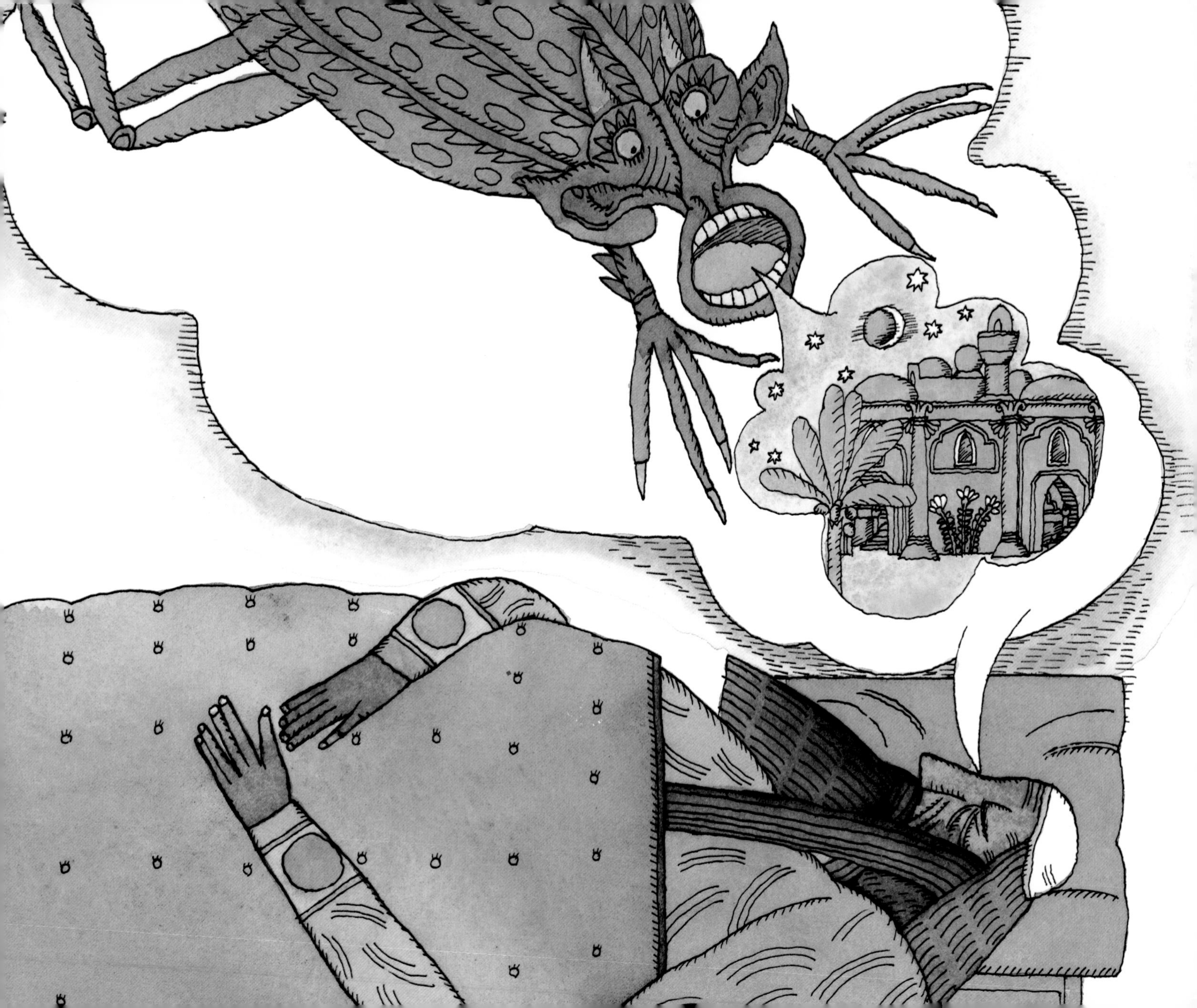

Every night Sorab lay awake, watching the moon get smaller and its light get dimmer. He became more and more afraid that the dream would come true.

So one Thursday morning Sorab went to town and sold his house and his lands to a rich merchant for thirteen bags of coins. He took the coins and went to a jeweler. Sorab looked at sapphires and diamonds. Then he saw a ruby as big as a pigeon's egg. He bought the giant ruby. The jeweler placed it in the center of Sorab's tall hat.

Sorab went to the harbor and found a ship that was going to a faraway land.

"All I have now is this one ruby," thought Sorab. "By the time Joseph finds out what I've done and where I've gone, I will be far away." As the ship sailed away, Sorab shouted, "*Now* let the moon grow dim! All I have will never go to him!"

But the ship was barely out to sea when a great storm blew up. The ship struck the rocks and began to sink. Sorab was swept overboard. He was never seen again. His hat flew off and hit the mast. Out popped the giant ruby, and it fell into the sea.

On Friday Joseph went to the market as usual. He heard a fisherman call, "Who will buy this large and beautiful fish?"

Deborah the weaver told the fisherman, "Here comes Joseph Who Loves the Sabbath. He will buy your fish, if anyone will."

When Joseph saw the big fish, he cried, "This is surely the finest fish in all the world!" He spent his last coin to buy it for the Sabbath.

Joseph went home. He baked the fish in the oven. At sundown he lit the Sabbath lamps and said the blessing. He set the Sabbath fish on the table and cut it open. Joseph saw something sparkling inside. It was a giant ruby! The fish had swallowed Sorab's ruby as it fell to the bottom of the sea.

After the Sabbath, Joseph took the ruby to town. He sold it back to the jeweler. He had just enough money to buy Sorab's house and lands.

The next Friday Joseph invited all his friends, and even strangers from the market, to share the Sabbath. Everyone came and ate the finest food. They said the blessings and sang songs.

And the home of Joseph Who Loved the Sabbath was filled with joy.

Special thanks to Dr. Isaiah Gafni, Senior Lecturer, Department of Jewish History, the Hebrew University, and to Dr. Leonard Singer Gold, Chief, Jewish Division, The New York Public Library.

About the Story

The source of "Joseph Who Loved the Sabbath," *Yosef Mokir Shabbat*, is eight lines of Aramaic in the Babylonian Talmud (Tractate *Shabbat*, 119A), which ends with the aphorism "He who lends to the Sabbath, the Sabbath repays him." The tale has been collected in the Arabian *A Thousand and One Nights* as "The Devout Israelite." It also belongs to world folklore, in which a great gem miraculously found in the belly of a fish is a recurring theme. Marilyn Hirsh based this retelling on Emanuel bin Gorion's *Mimekor Yisrael: Classical Jewish Folktales.*

About the Sabbath

In Joseph's life of poverty and crushing hard work, the opportunity to rest one day a week was most welcome, a custom unknown in much of the ancient world. But the Sabbath has always been more than a "Day of Rest." It is also a holy day, based on the Biblical Fourth Commandment—"Remember the Sabbath Day and keep it holy"—a day of spiritual renewal. In modern times, too, the Sabbath is a time to put aside the everyday concerns of getting and spending, to share the Sabbath peace with family and friends. Like all Jewish holidays, it begins at sundown and ends twenty-five hours later, when three stars appear in the sky. The Sabbath is greeted with the best one has. The spirit of Joseph's love for the Sabbath represents an ideal celebration.